SUBWAY SPARROW

SUBWAY SPARROW

Leyla Torres

Farrar · Straus · Giroux

New York

At the Atlantic Avenue station in Brooklyn, a sparrow flew into a subway car on the D train.

"Little bird, what are you doing down here?"

 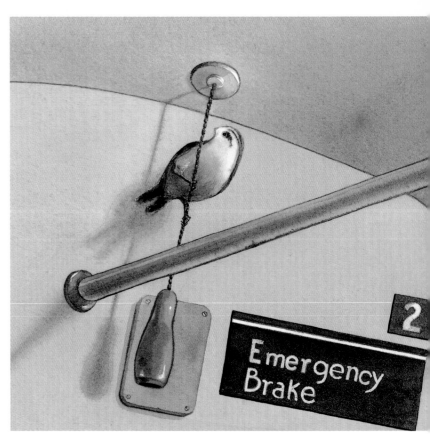

With a rumble, the train began to move.

"It's okay, it's okay—don't be afraid. I want to help you."

"¿Y esto? ¡Un pajarito en el metro!"

"Mister, maybe you can catch him with your hat..."

"Sí, con mi sombrero tal vez lo atajemos."

"If I go that way, maybe he'll fly toward you."
"Sí, ¡corre! ¡corre!"
The train rocked back and forth as it gained
speed.

"Hey, there's a bird in here!"

"I'll help, but my hands are so big, I might hurt him."

"¡Ay, se nos voló otra vez!"

"Oh no, he's off again!"

"O jejku, co ty wróbelku robisz w pociągu?"

"We're slowing down! Let's catch him before
the crowd gets on the train."

"Quizá con mi sombrilla."

"Nie dotykaj go parasolem!"

"No, forget the umbrella—it might hurt him."

"Moja apaszka."
"Yeah, cover him with the scarf!"
"Sí, cubrámoslo."
"Hurry, I'll pick him up."

The doors of the subway car closed. With a hiss, the train pulled away from the platform.

"His heart is beating so quickly ... He's so
soft, like a little cloud in my hands."

"Adios, pajarito."
"Good luck!"
"Do widzenia."
"Bye, little one."

For Juan

Grateful acknowledgment is made to the Metropolitan Transportation Authority
for permission to use their logo.
Library of Congress catalog card number: 97-55104
Published simultaneously in Canada by HarperCollins*CanadaLtd*
Color separations by Hong Kong Scanner Craft
Printed and bound in the United States of America by Berryville Graphics
Designed by Martha Rago. First edition, 1993